ZONDERKIDZ

Shoebox Sam
Copyright © 2011 by Mary Brigid Barrett Groth
Illustrations © 2011 by Frank Morrison

Requests for information should be addressed to:
Zonderkidz, Grand Rapids, Michigan 49530

Library of Congress Cataloging-in-Publication Data

Barrett, Mary Brigid.
    Shoebox Sam / by Mary Brigid Barrett ; illustrated by Frank Morrison.
      p. cm.
    Summary: On Saturdays, Delia and Jesse help Shoebox Sam, who teaches them
about charity and love by not only repairing shoes for paying customers, but also giving
poor and homeless people the dignity—and footwear—they need.
    ISBN 978-0-310-71549-8 (hardcover)
   [1. Shoes—Fiction. 2 Charity—Fiction 3. Homeless persons—Fiction. 4. Christian Life—
Fiction.] I. Morrison, Frank, 1971- ill. II. Title.
PZ7.B275343Sho 2011
[E]—dc22
                                          2009037509

Editor: Barbara Herndon
Art direction and design: Kris Nelson

Printed in China

11 12 13 14 15 /LPC/ 10 9 8 7 6 5 4 3 2 1

In loving memory of my father, Dr. James Patrick Barrett, who despite
every challenge and limitation, continued giving of himself to others.
—MBB

To Randerta Ward Evans.
Thank you for your generosity, wisdom, and guidance.
—FM

Shoebox Sam

Written by Mary Brigid Barrett

Illustrated by Frank Morrison

ZONDERVAN.com/
AUTHORTRACKER
follow your favorite authors

Shoebox Sam lives atop his shop on the corner of Magnolia and Vine. He shines old shoes and builds new soles. He shines them up fine. "Like new, but better," he tells us, "'cause new shoes walk tight, but old shoes walk light, like steppin' on a granny's feather bed."

Saturdays, we meet and greet him. "Mornin' Delia, Jesse," says Shoebox Sam. "I been waitin' for you children." He hands me a paper sack. I smell cinnamon crullers and fresh bread.

Shoebox Sam jiggles his keys in one hand, carries an old suitcase in the other. He opens the shop door. Delia turns on the lights. I plop the sack on the counter, and Sam swings his case up next to it. "Got us some fine shoebox shoes today, children," he says, tapping on the suitcase.

We nod and smile, bopping across the floor in our treadless sneakers, humming a foot-tapping hum. Shoebox Sam smiles an eye-crinkling, skin-wrinkling grin. "Shoes ain't rightly got a chance to grow old on you children," says Sam. "You'll wear those shoes out with pure delight!"

Shoebox Sam snaps his cleaning cloth and, humming our hum, sashays over to his display case, dusting and polishing it 'til it glistens and gleams. He brews coffee. We set out a plate of doughnuts. Sam places one red rose next to the doughnuts. "Stop and smell the roses," says Shoebox Sam. And we do, all three of us.

"Mmmm, hmmm," says Shoebox Sam. "Brings to mind the lovely Miss Lucratia Lavidia. She always wore attar of roses."

"The famous ballerina," I say.

"The very one," says he.

"The famous ballerina whose dancin' shoes you sewed and fixed."

"The very one," says he.

"And these are her shoes, hangin' right here on this pink ribbon."

"The very ones," says Shoebox Sam.

Delia reaches up to touch the dancing shoes, slowly running her fingers down the sides of the silken pink slippers. I close my eyes. I see the lovely Miss Lucratia Lavidia swirling 'round, high on her toes. I think I smell attar of roses. "What happened to Miss Lucratia?" I ask. "How come she never picked up her slippers?"

"How come," asked Delia, "you keep them here hanging on this wall?"

"Sometimes," says Shoebox Sam, winking at Delia, "it's better to remain a man of mystery."

Sam opens his suitcase, pulling out pairs of used shoes. The shoes are mended and polished and fixed up with new laces. I run to get boxes. Delia fetches a stack of tissue. We fold the paper in the boxes, tucking a pair of shoes in each. On the lids, Delia plants a sticker—red for the men's, green for the women's. I mark every box with the shoe size and color. We put the filled boxes on a back shelf.

A bell jingles. The door opens. "Good mornin', Doc. Your shoes will be ready momentarily," says Sam. "Children, why don't you get Doc a cup of coffee?"

The bell jingles. The door opens and a man shuffles in. His eyes dart 'round the room.

"Excuse me a minute, Doc," says Shoebox Sam. "Come in, sir. Sit right down. Children, get this gentleman a cup of coffee while he waits."

The man sits down. We give him coffee. He takes two doughnuts and eats them up fast. He takes one more. He drinks all the cream. He eats another doughnut.

Doc pays Sam, thanks him, and leaves. We watch the man take another doughnut. Delia tugs at Sam's sleeve. "That man has eaten near a half dozen doughnuts," she whispers.

"When you're hungry, you eat," says he.

Stooping, Sam looks at the man's shoes. "These shoes need a might lot of work," he says. "Jesse, please get this customer a size ten replacement 'til I can mend his shoes. And, Delia, isn't this the week we're givin' away complimentary socks?"

I run to the shelf and pull out a box with a red sticker, marked 10-BROWN. Delia fetches a new pair of socks. I open the box and unfold the tissue. "These suit you, sir?" I ask.

The man nods. Sam gently pulls off the man's ragged socks and puts on a new pair. Helping the man into his shoes, he laces them up.

The man stands and walks 'round the room. He shakes the hand of
the shoebox man.

At noontime, Sam puts bread and cheese on the table. We run out to play ball in the street. Customers come. Customers go. We make faces at Shoebox Sam through the window. He tap dances a pair of shoes against the pane. It begins to rain. We dash inside, shaking ourselves dry like wet puppies.

A lady comes in. She wants her high heels fixed. A man needs new rubber soles. A lady needs her purse straps sewn.

The doorbell jingles. An old woman comes in hunched over from the rain. She has no umbrella.

Delia taps Sam on the back. "She is wearin' at least five different dresses and four sweaters," she says.

"When you're cold, you cover up," says he.

"Let me get you some hot coffee, ma'am," says Delia, helping her onto a bench.

Sam makes her sandwiches. She eats two.

"Looks like you could use some dry shoes," he says.

I run back to the shelf. "What size?" I ask.

"About a six," says Sam.

I open the box for the lady and pull back the tissue.

"Do you have anything prettier?" she asks.

I give Shoebox Sam all the boxes marked 6. We open them up. "Not a pretty pair in the lot, ma'am," he says, "but serviceable and warm."

Sam helps the lady into the shoes. She pats his hand and gathers up her cart and bag. The pink slippers on the wall catch her eye. "Those shoes are the most beautiful shoes I've seen in all my life. They wouldn't be my size, would they?"

"Oh no, ma'am!" exclaims Delia. "Those are special shoes. You know, toe shoes, for a dancer."

"They belonged to Miss Lucratia Lavidia," I say. "A beautiful ballerina." The lady drags her cart across the floor. Caressing the shoes, she presses one silken slipper against her wrinkled cheek. With a wistful sigh, she walks away.

The shoebox man stops her. Into her hands, he places the beautiful dancing shoes of Miss Lucratia Lavidia.

The lady looks at the slippers. She removes one of her sweaters, wrapping it 'round the dancing shoes. Gently, she tucks them into her cart and takes her leave. Pausing in the doorway, she turns, her shoulders straight, her head high. "Thank you most kindly," she says.

"You are most kindly welcome," says the shoebox man.

Delia and I look at the wall, empty now.
We look at each other.

We run after the lady. I hand her the red
rose. "Attar of roses," I say. "Complimentary
with dancin' shoes today."

We skip back to the shoebox man, prancing through the puddles.
"What are you children doin' out in this wet?" says Shoebox Sam.
We laugh. "When you're happy, you dance!"